To Trent, for asking the question.

Library of Congress Cataloging-in-Publication Data available.

ISBN 978-1-4521-7992-6

Manufactured in China.

Design by Amelia Mack and Abbie Goveia.
Typeset in Capita.
The illustrations in this book were rendered in ink on paper and colored digitally.

10 9 8 7 6 5 4 3 2 1

Chronicle Books LLC
680 Second Street
San Francisco, California 94107

Chronicle Books—we see things differently.
Become part of our community at www.chroniclekids.com

What Color Is Night?

Grant Snider

chronicle books · san francisco

What color is night?

Is it only black . . .

and white?

Look closer.

The night is blue

with black shapes and lines

and a big yellow moon

beginning to rise.

The park aglow with gold fireflies

the silver streak

of a train rolling by.

Fat brown moths
dancing

in yellow streetlights

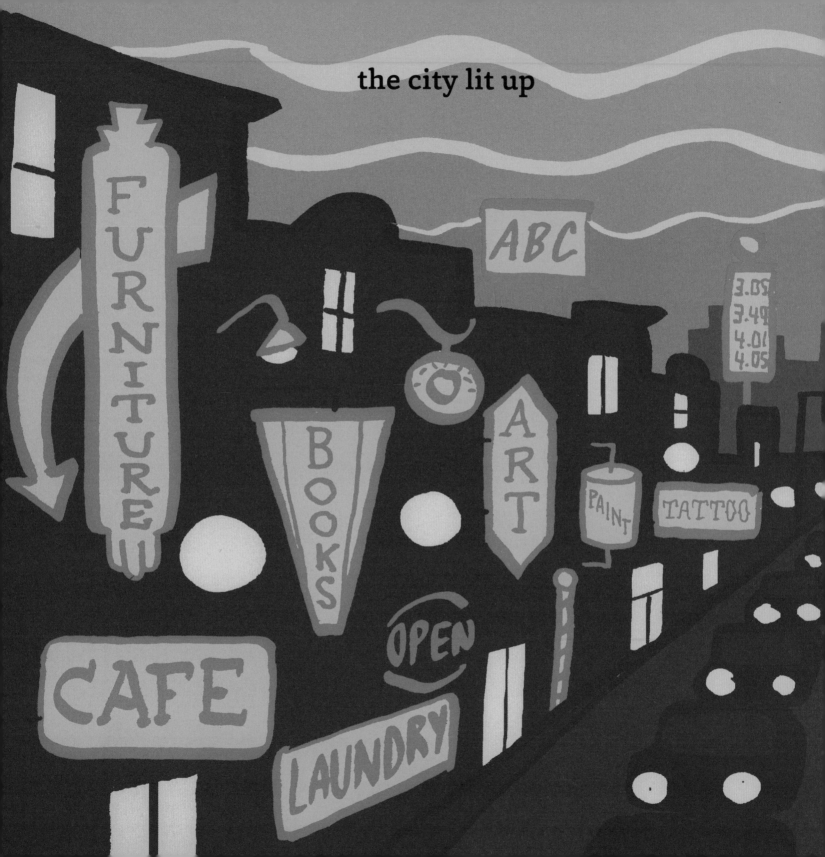

with neon red signs.

Yellow headlights
on a dark country road

a nighttime visit

a green-eyed glow.

A still blue pond

the white moon,
twice

a thousand silver stars
spilled across the sky.

One last orange window

houses of black

the gray face of a clock

a midnight snack.

And there,
in a sky of indigo

all the night's colors
in one moonbow.

A clear window

a silver moonbeam

pink and purple clouds

a night of good dreams

and colors unseen.